For Jason
—A.R.

Katherine Tegen Books is an imprint of HarperCollins Publishers.

The Great Pumpkin Contest
Copyright © 2019 by Angela Rozelaar

ISBN 978-0-06-274137-0

The artist used water-soluble crayons, gouache, and collage
to create the illustrations for this book.
Typography by Rachel Zegar
19   20   21   22   23   SCP   10   9   8   7   6   5   4   3   2   1
❖
First Edition

The GREAT Pumpkin Contest

Angie
Rozelaar

 KATHERINE TEGEN BOOKS
An Imprint of HarperCollins Publishers

The leaves were beginning to change color.
The air had become brighter and colder.
And with the change in seasons from summer to fall . . .
it was time for Cat County's Great Pumpkin Contest.

In this little county lived two cats as different as could be.

Mimi spent her days inside, reading stories about cats who were bold, smart, and loved.

Sometimes she wished she had a friend.

Clara preferred to be outside, tending
her garden and having tea parties.

Both wanted to win the first-prize ribbon in the Great Pumpkin Contest.

Earlier that summer, Mimi had read all the books.

Purr-fect Pumpkins

The Power of Meow

Green Paws

Plant Food

pumpkin seeds

pumpkin seeds

pumpkin seeds

And she formed a plan.

She found the sunniest spot in her garden, made sure it was away from the wind, added just the right plant foods, and then dug tiny holes and planted her pumpkin seeds.

She waited.

And waited.

And waited some more.

Until one day . . .

A tiny sprout had appeared! Soon there were vines.
And then flowers!

Next door, Clara had happily planted her pumpkin seeds all over her garden.

Before long, her pumpkin patch was filled with lots and lots of little pumpkins.

Clara peeked at Mimi's pumpkin patch. There was one pumpkin that was getting very big and round.

"Wow!" said Clara. "Your pumpkin looks AMAZING! How did you make it grow so big?"

"I've read lots of books," said Mimi.
"Very smart," said Clara. She went back to tend her
crop of little pumpkins.

Mimi's pumpkin continued to grow.

And grow . . .

and GROW!

Clara's pumpkins grew, too.

Soon it was time for the Great Pumpkin Contest, but how was Mimi going to get her enormous pumpkin to the fair?

She tried pushing it.

And pulling it.

But it was just no use.
The pumpkin was too BIG. If only there was another way.

Ta-da! A wheelbarrow! It was perfect.

Mimi rolled her gigantic pumpkin onto the cart and set off for the fairground.

She couldn't wait for everyone to admire her very big pumpkin.

Clara stacked up some of her beautiful little
pumpkins and headed to the fair, too.
She was also very proud.

The road into town was bumpy. The pumpkin wiggled and jiggled.

Soon Mimi's giant pumpkin began to tip.

It teetered and tottered and . . .

Look out for that pothole, Mimi!

rolled right out of that rickety cart with an enormous

THUNK!

SPLAT!

KABLOOEY!

The whole town was covered in Mimi's giant
gloopy, schloopy pumpkin.
Mimi was horrified. She ran back home and hid.

There were pumpkin guts everywhere! Who will ever want to be my friend now?

Later that day, Mimi heard a knock at her door.

It was Clara! "I brought you a pumpkin, even though it's not so big. Maybe next year you could show me your pumpkin-growing secrets," she said.

Mimi slowly smiled. "Yes, I would like that."

shopping
milk
sardines
cream
kibble
tuna
purritos
more cream

MEW
YORK

PURR-TH

HISSISSIPPI

MILK

Carving Ins·purr-ation

How to A-paw-logize

A TAIL OF TWO KITTIES

Mimi sat and stared at Clara's pumpkin.
And soon she formed a new plan.

The next day, Mimi went down to the fair.
She had a surprise just for Clara.

A first-prize pumpkin they could enjoy together—as friends.

The Life Cycle
of a Pumpkin

Pumpkin
Seeds

Sprout

Orange
Pumpkin

Green
Pumpkin

Flower

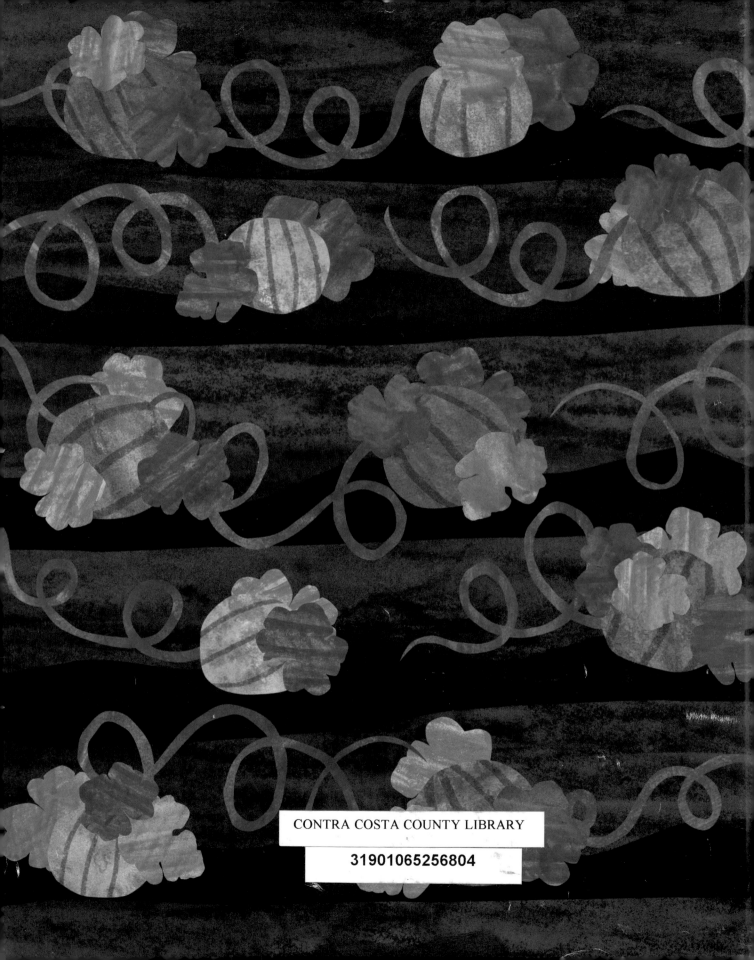